FANG THE DENTIST

by Mike Thaler • pictures by Jared Lee

Troll Associates

**For
Dr. Chuck,
defender of the tooth.
M.T.**

**To P.J., Jana, and Jennifer
who always keep me smiling.
J.L.**

Library of Congress Cataloging-in-Publication Data

Thaler, Mike, (date)
    Fang the dentist / by Mike Thaler; pictures by Jared Lee.
      p.   cm.—(Funny Firsts)
    Summary: After hearing family members describe root canals, capped
teeth, and drills, Snarvey Gooper becomes fearful about going to the
dentist.
    ISBN 0-8167-3020-2 (lib. bdg.)   ISBN 0-8167-3021-0 (pbk.)
    [1. Dental care—Fiction.] I. Lee, Jared D., ill. II. Title.
III. Series.
PZ7.T3Fan 1994
[E]—dc20   93-18594

I have to go to the dentist.

Mom says I need my teeth checked.

My teeth are *fine*.

I brushed them a month ago.

Mom says the dentist will clean them with special machines.

Dad says he has a drill . . .

and an assistant.

Sis says he has a special chair,

and lots of lights,

and equipment.

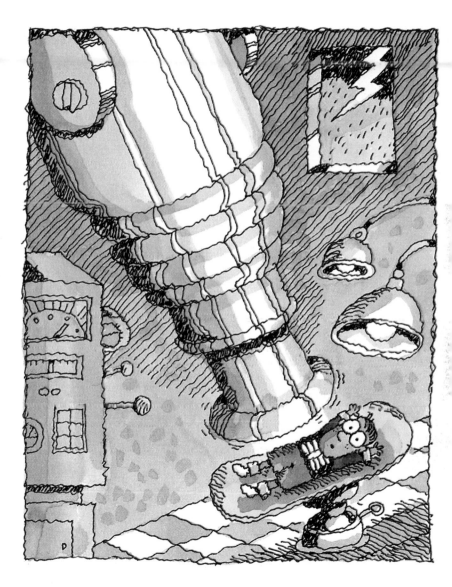

Uncle Bob says he gives him a shot

and, sometimes, he gives him gas.

I'm not sure I want to go.

Aunt Esther had her
bottom teeth capped.

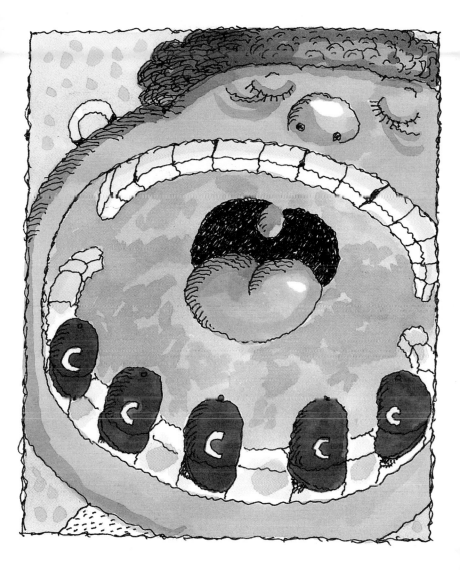

Grandma had a whole bridge put in.

Sis had a tooth pulled,

and Uncle Bob had a whole root canal.

Now ships can sail through his mouth.

I'm *really* not sure I want to go.

But it's Friday at three,
and I *have* to go!

I bid farewell to my hamster.

Mom takes me in the car.

We finally get to the dentist's office.

The room is filled with victims.

The nurse calls out their names
and, one by one, they disappear.

Finally, she calls my name,
"Snarvey Gooper?"
"That's me! It's my turn!!"

She takes me to a room

and closes the door.

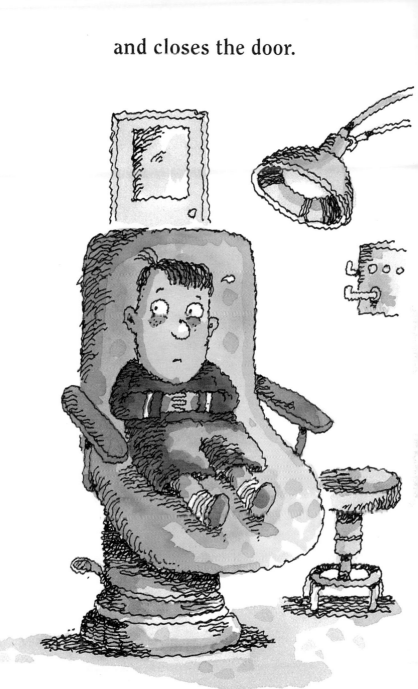

The dentist comes in.
He looks at every tooth.

He smiles.
He tells me to brush every day.
Then, he gives me . . .

a rubber spider and a new toothbrush!

I can't wait to go to the dentist again!